DISNEY
FROZEN II

Adapted by Emily Skwish
Illustrated by Art Mawhinney

we make books come alive®
pi kids **Phoenix International Publications, Inc.**
Chicago • London • New York • Hamburg • Mexico City • Sydney

King Agnarr tells the best bedtime stories—especially if you like intense tales with lots of fighting. Fortunately, young Anna and Elsa like all kinds of stories. This one happens to be about the day their father became King of Arendelle during a clash with the Northuldra. "The past has a way of returning," the king warns. Nighty-night!

While the sisters fall asleep, look around the cozy bedroom for some reminders of the past:

Arendellian shield

this wall hanging

this book

this painting

this portrait of King Runeard

Queen Iduna's scarf

Many years later, Elsa is Queen of Arendelle. She begins hearing a voice, one that only she can hear. It calls her out of the castle, and it speaks to a part of her that no one has ever connected with before. As she listens, she reaches out to the voice with her magic. To Elsa's surprise, beautiful figures made of snow and ice form all around her. They could be the keys to Arendelle's past—and future.

Spot these crystalline creations:

 ice wind-swirl

 ice giant

 ice salamander

 ice water-horse

 this ice tree   this ice tree

Elsa, Anna, Kristoff, Olaf, and Sven approach a mist-covered forest and discover four large monoliths, each with an ancient symbol representing one of the four elements: Earth, Fire, Water, and Wind. No one knows what secrets and adventures await in this enchanted place.

Search the scene for these mist-ical things:

 this flower

 this flower

 this plant

 this plant

 fire symbol

 wind symbol

In the forest, the friends are introduced to the spirits of nature. The Wind Spirit makes an entrance that blows them away. Now they are stuck in a swirling vortex that has them spinning, twisting, and feeling more than a little sick.

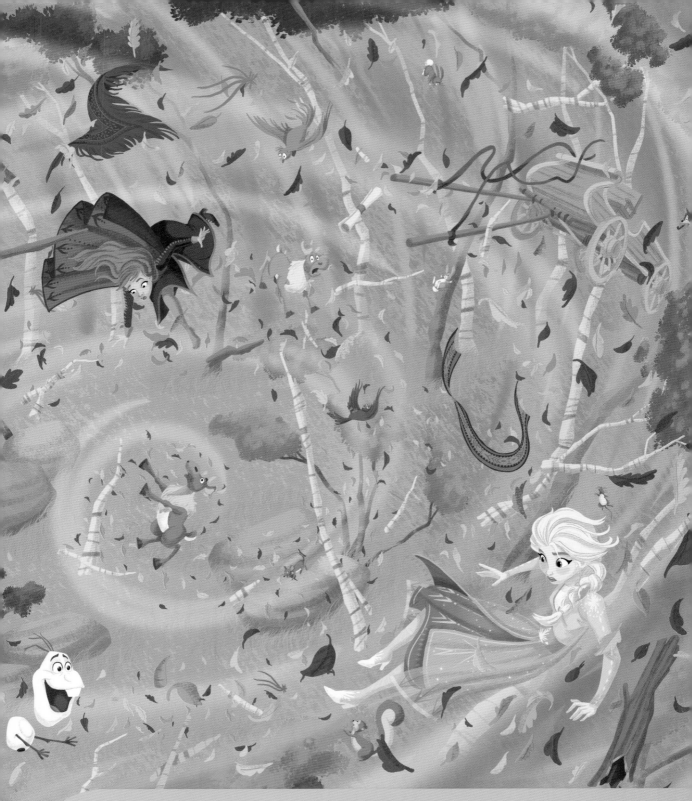

It's tricky to hold it together inside the vortex. Help the friends find these things that have spun away:

Kristoff's ring

Anna's boot

Kristoff's belt

Sven's harness

Queen Iduna's scarf

Olaf's nose

On the journey, Elsa and her friends meet the Northuldra, an ancient, nomadic people. They also meet several Arendellian soldiers who have been trapped along with the Northuldra in the Enchanted Forest for thirty-four years. Suddenly, the Fire Spirit arrives on the scene. This excitable amphibian is a real trail blazer. As it scurries, it leaves a fiery path that threatens to send the forest up in flames!

Can you keep your cool as you find these people of Northuldra and Arendelle?

Yelena

Honeymaren

Ryder

Mattias

this Northuldra
soldier

this Northuldra
soldier

As the friends learn more about the history of the Northuldra, they are discovered by Earth Giants. These behemoths sense Elsa's magic in the air, and they come sniff-sniff-sniffing to find her. Elsa quickly steps in to create a diversion that sends the Earth Giants on their lumbering way.

It's a giant task, but you can do it! Find these tiny things:

 this red squirrel

 this shrew

 this lemming

 this otter

 this arctic fox

 this hedgehog

Elsa knows that the journey to discover the secrets of her power will be dangerous. She creates an ice boat for Anna and Olaf and sends them away from her, to safety. The only problem is, Anna accidentally steers them past a riverbank where the Earth Giants are taking their afternoon nap.

As Anna and Olaf row their boat gently—very, very gently—down the stream, locate these dreaming Giants:

Elsa sets out on her own to find the secret of her power, and she encounters another force of nature, the Water Spirit. Is it a fish? A whale? No, the Water Nokk is a majestic horse that embodies the power of water. Elsa must earn its respect before it will let her reach her destination.

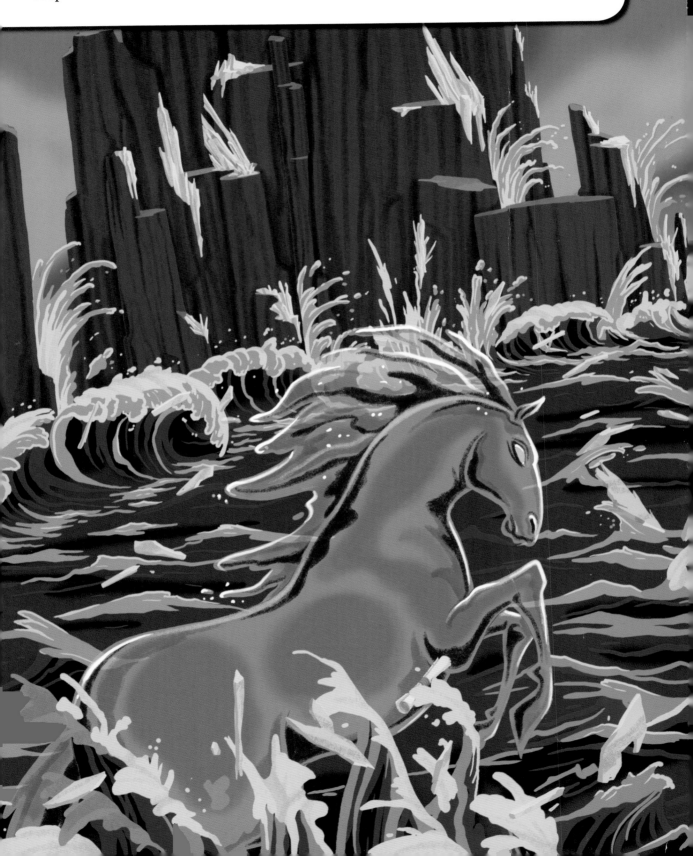

Dive in and find these icy blasts:

Tiptoe back to the bedtime story and search for these items that foreshadow the future:

this book

this drawing of Olaf

ship in a bottle

Elsa's gloves

this toy reindeer

this painting

Skate back to Elsa's icy creations and collect these shimmering crystals before they melt:

Journey back to the monoliths and find this fantastical foliage:

Blow back to the Wind Spirit and catch these spiraling things:

this tree

this bird

sleigh

this reindeer

this log

Anna's book

Blaze a trail back to the Fire Spirit and find these things that will *not* go up in smoke today:

this scarf

this vine

this tree

this tree

this tree

this belt

Thunder back to the Earth Giants and find these other examples of magic at work:

Wind Spirit

this snowflake

this ice crystal

this snowflake

Fire Spirit

this snowflake

There's something fishy about the river. Slip back to the ice boat and find these splishy and splashy things:

Swim (or gallop) back to the Water Spirit and identify these rugged rock formations:

Queen Iduna kept notes on parchment as she searched for clues to Elsa's power. Can you find 20 of her scrolls hidden throughout this book?